Willy Whitefeather's

Outdoor
SURVIVAL
HANDBOOK
for KIDS

HARBINGER HOUSE
TUCSON

HARBINGER HOUSE, INC.
Tucson, Arizona

Manufactured in the United States of America

10 9 8 7 6 5 4 3

∞ This book was printed on acid-free, archival-quality paper.
Illustrations by Willy Whitefeather
Art Direction by Nancy J. Parker

Library of Congress Cataloging-in-Publication Data

Whitefeather, Willy, 1935–
Willy Whitefeather's outdoor survival handbook for kids.
Summary: The author advises young people on how to
survive being lost or stranded in the woods or desert.
1. Wilderness survival — Juvenile literature.
[1. Wilderness survival. 2. Survival] I. Title.
GV200.5.W47   1990   613.6'9   89-26929
ISBN 0-943173-47-7 (alk. paper)

A LOT OF BOYS AND GIRLS
HAVE GOTTEN LOST OUT IN THE
DESERT, WOODS, AND MOUNTAINS
AND NEVER RETURNED —
          'CAUSE NO GROWN-UP EVER
          SHOWED 'EM WHAT TO DO...
I WROTE THIS BOOK FOR MY
GRANDCHILDREN AND FOR
          ALL YOU KIDS
SO YOU'LL MAKE IT BACK **SAFE**.

Willy WHITEFEATHER
88

Dear Kids,

I've lived deep in The woods for many years, building my own log cabins, cooking wild food over camp-fires, and Talking with my neighbors, The black bears.

But Willy has taught me a bunch of ways to get along in The outdoors I never Knew. I love his book—it's filled with great stuff and it's fun!!

Linda Runyon

MORE ABOUT LINDA ON THE LAST PAGE.

WHAT'S IN THIS BOOK

MORE of WHAT'S IN THIS BOOK

KIDS, WHEN YOU LEAVE YOUR HOUSE, YOU'RE **OUTDOORS.** ANYTIME YOU'RE OUTSIDE AWAY FROM HOME, BE READY FOR A **CHANGE IN THE WEATHER.** IT'S BEST TO **ALWAYS BE READY** AND NEVER TAKE OUR MOTHER EARTH FOR GRANTED *Hi* SO IT'S BEST ALWAYS TO **RELY ON YOURSELF.**

THIS BOOK WILL GIVE YOU **CONFIDENCE,** AND HELP YOU WHEN YOU GET LOST, SO YOU WILL **MAKE IT BACK** TO YOUR CAMP OR YOUR HOME IN GOOD SHAPE.

LET'S WATCH *TINA* AND *DOOLEY* AND SEE WHAT THEY DO WHEN THEY WANDER... TOO FAR FROM CAMP AND GET CAUGHT OUTDOORS WITHOUT THE RIGHT CLOTHING OR EQUIPMENT.

YOU ARE NEVER LOST!

MOM AND DAD, THE HOUSE, THE CAR MAY BE LOST, BUT **YOU** ARE **RIGHT HERE!**

JUST REMEMBER TO **MARK YOUR** SCRATCH LIKE THIS ⟩⟩→ ·········· EVERY **TIME** YOU GO AWAY FROM CAMP—SO YOU CAN FIND **YOUR WAY BACK** - OR THEY CAN FIND YOU.

CAN YOU SEE YOUR TRAIL?

⟩⟩⟩→ AND **REMEMBER** ←⟨⟨

BEFORE YOU WANDER OUT OF CAMP **ALWAYS TELL SOMEONE**, OR *LEAVE A NOTE* — EVEN IF YOU GO OFF MAD. AND TAKE A *WHISTLE* 'CAUSE YELLING DOESN'T GO FAR IN THE WOODS. **LOUD WHISTLES** DO!

2

DOOLEY IS IN THE WOODS. THE GROUND IS COVERED WITH LEAVES AND BRUSH, SO AS HE WALKS ALONG, HE PICKS UP STICKS THAT ARE ABOUT **HALF AS LONG** AS HIS **ARM** AND ABOUT **AS BIG AROUND AS HIS LITTLE FINGER.** DOOLEY CRACKS ONE IN **HALF,** SO THE STICK MAKES A  'V' AND HOLDS TOGETHER IN **ONE PIECE.**

DOOLEY WALKS ALONG AND PUTS A V-STICK ON THE GROUND **POINTING THE WAY HE'S GOING,** THEN LOOKS BACK ONCE IN A WHILE AND WHEN HE CAN **HARDLY** SEE THE LAST V-STICK, HE PUTS DOWN **ANOTHER** V-STICK TO FIND HIS WAY **BACK** TO CAMP.

"UH-OH! I THINK I'M **LOST**," SAYS TINA. "IT'S **OKAY**," SAYS DOOLEY, "WHEN WE LEFT CAMP, I GRABBED THIS **LONG STICK** AND I'VE BEEN **SCRATCHING THE GROUND** WITH IT. WE CAN FOLLOW THE SCRATCH **BACK TO CAMP!**"

I'M LOST TOO

STONE PILES

ARE USED IN THE DESERT AND MOUNTAINS TO **MARK TRAILS.** DOOLEY DRAGS HIS WALKING STICK TO **SCRATCH THE EARTH,** BUT IF IT **RAINS** OR **SNOWS,** THAT COULD **WIPE** OUT THE SCRATCH MARK, SO TINA MAKES A **SMALL STONE PILE** LIKE THIS. TINA LOOKS BACK ONCE IN A WHILE - AND WHEN SHE CAN **HARDLY SEE** THE LAST STONE PILE, SHE MAKES A **NEW ONE** TO MARK HER TRAIL **BACK TO CAMP.** AND THAT WAY...

SEE PAGE 55 ON PICKING UP A ROCK

TINY →
LITTLE →
LITTLER →
LITTLER →
BIG ROCK

LIZARD HELPER

WW

... A SEARCH PARTY CAN FIND *THEM!*

5

Mom says, "You kids were smart to drag that stick to find your way back to camp, but now we have a problem. There's a SNOWSTORM coming and the car has a dead battery!"

DOOLEY REMEMBERED TO SAVE SOME **PLASTIC BAGS** FROM THE GROCERY STORE'S FRUIT AND **VEGETABLE** DEPARTMENT.

KIDS! KEEP **ALL** PLASTIC BAGS AWAY FROM YOUR NOSE AND MOUTH AND FROM THE LITTLE KIDS, THEY ARE NOT FOR **PLAY**—BUT THEY CAN SAVE YOUR LIFE!

TO KEEP HIS **FEET WARM** AND **DRY,** DOOLEY PUTS A PLASTIC BAG **OVER EACH** BARE FOOT,

THEN HE PUTS ON HIS SOCKS,

THEN HE PUTS ON ANOTHER PLASTIC BAG **OVER EACH SOCK,**

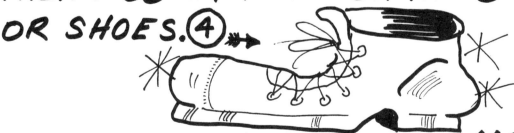

THEN DOOLEY PUTS ON HIS BOOTS OR SHOES.④

NOW DOOLEY'S FEET ARE **WARM** AND **SAFE** FROM **WATER.** WET FEET IN SNOW COULD MEAN **FROSTBITE!**

DOOLEY ALSO THOUGHT TO BRING 4 LARGE (30 GALLON SIZE) PLASTIC TRASH BAGS. HE THEN CUTS 3 HOLES IN ONE FOR HIS HEAD AND ARMS TO FIT THRU.

HE TAKES THE NEXT 2 BAGS AND HE WRAPS HIS LEGS WITH THEM AND THEN HE TIES THEM WITH SOME STRING.

THEN DOOLEY

Hi, MOM!

PLASTIC BAG

*TIE STRING NOT REAL TIGHT

PUTS HIS CLOTHES ON OVER ALL THE PLASTIC BAGS. NOW DOOLEY CUTS 3 HOLES IN THE LAST BAG TO PUT HIS HEAD AND ARMS THRU, AND HE PUTS IT ON OVER HIS CLOTHES FOR WHEN IT RAINS OR SNOWS. PLASTIC BAGS ARE ONE OF THE BEST WAYS TO HOLD IN YOUR BODY HEAT FAST AND KEEP YOU WARM AND DRY WHEN IT GETS COLD.

9

TINA ALSO PUTS A CLEAR PLASTIC BAG **OVER EACH HAND.** ⟶ SHE PUSHES THE BAG DOWN OVER HER FINGERS...

THEN TINA PUTS ON HER GLOVES OR MITTENS.

NOW TINA'S HANDS ARE **SAFE FROM SNOW OR WATER.** THE PLASTIC BAG SEALS IN IN HER BODY HEAT—LIKE SEALSKIN DOES FOR THE ESKIMO PEOPLE.

SAVE THE SEALS!

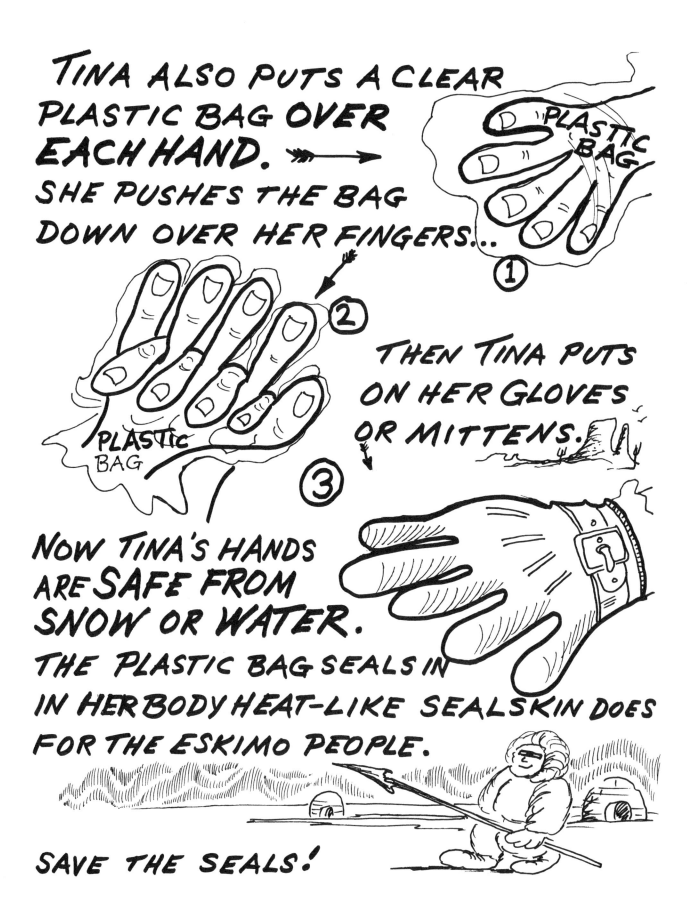

10

THERMAL
AREA

BODY HEAT,

YEP! DOOLEY KNOWS THAT MOST OF YOUR BODY HEAT IS LOST THRU THE TOP OF YOUR HEAD, SO DOOLEY PUTS ON A WOOL CAP. IN COLD WEATHER, COVER THE TOP OF YOUR HEAD, DAY AND NIGHT, SO YOU'LL BE WARMER AND SLEEP WARMER. PUT ON A WOOL SWEATER TO KEEP YOUR THERMAL AREA WARM TOO. TO KEEP YOUR FACE WARM, WEAR A SKI MASK. IF YOU DON'T HAVE ONE, SMEAR VASELINE ™ OR OIL ON YOUR FACE AGAINST FROSTBITE.

TINA'S SKI MASK

11

THE SNOWSTORM OR BLIZZARD COMES ON FAST, SO THERE'S NOT MUCH TIME. DŌŌLEY'S MOM DOESN'T HAVE A SHOVEL, SO SHE PULLS OFF A **SUN VISOR** FROM THE CAR, OR A **HUBCAP**. THE VISOR THEN BECOMES A **SHOVEL** TO DIG A **SNOW CAVE**...

DŌŌLEY AND TINA HELP MOM, USING A **HUBCAP** AND A **DIGGING STICK**, 'CAUSE IF THEY USE JUST THEIR HANDS, THEY COULD GET **TOO COLD.**

FIRST, THEY DIG A **CRAWL-IN HOLE**, THEN THEY **SCOOP OUT** A **SNOW CAVE** BIG ENOUGH FOR THEM TO FIT IN EASY LIKE THIS. ⟶

SNOW BANK

BAMMO WHAM WHAP

CRAWL-IN HOLE ⟶

SIDE VIEW

PACK PACK PACK
PACK PACK
PACK PACK
PACK

SNOW BENCH

AND THEN THEY USE THE **SUN VISOR**, **HUBCAP**, A **FLAT ROCK** OR A **CHUNK** OF **TREE BARK** TO **PACK** THE SNOW GENTLY, SO THE CAVE WON'T CAVE IN ON THEM. ONCE INSIDE, THEY TAKE TURNS **WARMING** EACH OTHER'S **HANDS** AND **FEET:** HANDS UNDER **ARMPITS,** FEET AGAINST **STOMACH.**

AHHHH

OOOF

WHEN THE SNOWSTORM FINALLY REACHES THEM, THE WIND GETS REALLY COLD. IT'S *BELOW FREEZING*. DEEP INSIDE THEIR SNOW CAVE, MOM, DOOLEY, AND TINA ARE **WARM AND SAFE** FROM THE COLD ICY WIND. DOOLEY HAS BROUGHT IN A STICK **TO KEEP AN AIR HOLE OPEN**, 'CAUSE THEY'VE **CLOSED OFF** THE CRAWL-IN HOLE WITH SNOW TO KEEP THE **COLD** WIND **OUT**.

POW WHACK

ICY WIND

STICK LONG ENOUGH TO GO THRU SNOW **AND THEN SOME**

AIR HOLE

HOW'D THAT RABBIT GET IN HERE?

CRAWL-IN HOLE CLOSED WITH SNOW

WILLY DID IT

IF DOOLEY AND HIS FAMILY HAD STAYED IN THE CAR, THEY MIGHT HAVE **FROZEN**. A 2-FOOT THICK SNOW CAVE WALL IS A **WHOLE LOT** BETTER THAN A SKINNY CAR WINDOW BETWEEN YOU AND A BLIZZARD.

TINA TIES HER BRIGHT ORANGE BANDANNA ONTO THE STICK. THE **BRIGHT PIECE OF CLOTH** CAN BE **SEEN** BY ANYONE LOOKING FOR THEM.

DOOLEY MOVES THE STICK **UP AND DOWN** TO KEEP THE AIR HOLE **OPEN** SO THEY HAVE AIR TO BREATHE.

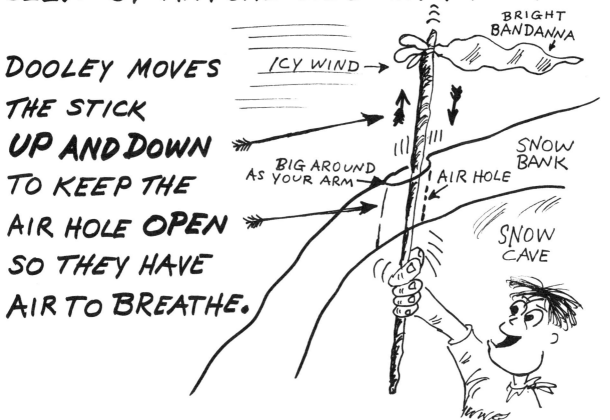

BRIGHT BANDANNA

ICY WIND →

BIG AROUND AS YOUR ARM

AIR HOLE

SNOW BANK

SNOW CAVE

A COLD WIND IS BLOWING

TINA IS IN THE MOUNTAINS AND THERE'S NO SNOW FOR A SNOW CAVE, THERE'S NO ROCK CAVE AROUND, AND NO WHERE TO GET OUT OF THE WIND. TINA LOOKS FOR A BOULDER OR A LOG. SHE GOES TO THE NO-WIND SIDE AND, USING A SHARP ROCK, TINA DIGS A PIT BIG ENOUGH TO LIE DOWN IN AND ABOUT ONE ARM DEEP. SHE THROWS IN LEAVES OR DRY GRASS TO MAKE A BED, THEN BRANCHES ACROSS THE TOP, CRAWLS IN — IF HER FEET ARE COLD, SHE COVERS THEM WITH EARTH —

WHAT YOU SAY—WHAT YOU FEEL

CAN KEEP YOU ALIVE IF YOU ARE LOST IN THE WOODS OR DESERT IF YOU SAY...

I'M FREEZING!

THEN YOU ARE!
OR...
IF YOU SAY
I'M BURNING UP!

THEN YOU ARE! IT'S BEST TO SAY..."IT'S JUST RIGHT FOR THIS TIME OF DAY AND THIS TIME OF YEAR AND I AM IN BALANCE WITH IT." HERE'S A TIP—SAY IT'S HOT WHEN IT'S COLD AND IT'S COLD WHEN IT'S HOT—AND IF YOU BELIEVE IT, YOU WILL MAKE IT!

IT STARTS TO RAIN

DŌŌLEY IS LOST IN THE WOODS.

HE SEES THE BIG GRAY RAINCLOUDS COMING. HE PUTS ON HIS RAINCOAT OR HIS PLASTIC GARBAGE BAG WITH THE 3 HOLES CUT OUT FOR HIS HEAD AND ARMS. THEN DOOLEY TAKES OFF HIS SHOES AND PULLS A SMALL PLASTIC VEGETABLE BAG ON OVER HIS SOCKS TO KEEP HIS FEET AND SOCKS DRY. HE PUTS HIS SHOES BACK ON—AND THEN HE LOOKS FOR COVER UNTIL THE STORM GOES BY. WET CLOTHES ARE NOT GOOD TO HAVE ON WHEN NIGHT TIME COMES. AAAAHHHHHHHCHOOOÕŌ!

LONG AGO, THE CHEROKEES LIVED IN CAVES IN THE SMOKY MOUNTAINS. A CAVE IS GREAT IN A

RAIN STORM!
IT'S BEST NOT TO GO
WAY DEEP INSIDE THE CAVE,
BUT STAY NEAR THE ENTRANCE
AND STAY DRY UNTIL IT STOPS RAINING.
BEARS AND WOLVES AND MOUNTAIN LIONS
LIKE CAVES TOO. A ROCK OVERHANG IS
BEST FOR A LOST KID.
      DOOLEY LOOKS TO

YEP!

SEE WHERE THE BIRDS AND
ANIMALS GO WHEN IT RAINS—BIRDS GO
UNDER THE THICK TREE BRANCHES,
DEER GO UNDER THE BIG TREES,
BADGERS AND PRAIRIE DOGS GO INTO
A HOLE IN THE GROUND, AND COYOTES
GO INTO A DEN. FROGS DON'T CARE
IF IT RAINS OR NOT —

YAHHHHH
WHAP

IF YOU ARE A FROG, FORGET THIS PAGE!

DURING A **LIGHTNING STORM**, GET **AWAY** FROM A **HILLTOP** OR ANY **TREE BY ITSELF**, OR AN **OPEN MEADOW**.

BOOM ZAP

ZAP BOOM

YIKE! YIKE! YIKE!

NO

NO

YES

YES

YEP

YEP

WHEN DOOLEY SEES LIGHTNING, HE GETS INTO A **GROVE OF TREES** OR GETS DOWN **BETWEEN BOULDERS**, OR **NEXT TO A CLIFF WALL**, OR **LAYS DOWN** IF HE'S IN THE OPEN—TILL IT'S OVER. TALK FROM YOUR HEART TO THE LIGHTNING. DON'T BE AFRAID.

20

DOOLEY AND FRIENDS, WAITING OUT THE RAIN

SEE THE ANIMALS

WHEN YOU ARE OUTDOORS, YOU ARE A GUEST IN THE ANIMALS' HOME. BE CALM, LOOK AROUND YOU, AND THINK. AN ANIMAL KNOWS WHEN YOU ARE AFRAID. SO TALK TO THE ANIMALS AS THE OLD CHEROKEES DO — SAY, "OH-SEE-OH, DOO-HEET-SOO?" WHICH MEANS "HELLO, HOW ARE YOU?"

SOME ANIMALS WILL BE AFRAID OF YOU AND RUN AWAY. SOME ANIMALS CAN'T SEE VERY FAR. SO STAND VERY STILL. MOST ANIMALS HAVE GOOD NOSES AND THEY CAN SMELL YOU IF THE WIND IS BLOWING FROM YOU TO THEM — THEY HAVE GOOD EARS AND THEY CAN HEAR YOU WALKING.

SEE THE BEAR

SEE THE BABY BEAR? *OORG*

IF YOU TRY TO PET THE **BABY** BEAR, **MAMA** BEAR WILL **PET YOU!** THIS IS A CORNER. IF YOU SEE AN ANIMAL OR A SNAKE IN HERE, **WALK AWAY** - BUT **LOOK** WHERE YOU **WALK!** IF YOU SEE A **MAMA** ANIMAL, THEN **PAPA** IS CLOSE BY. IF AN ANIMAL **WALKS SLOWLY** AT YOU, IT MAY BE SICK WITH **RABIES,** SO GET AWAY FROM IT— **FAST!**

ROWRG

IF THE ANIMAL IS **RUNNING AT YOU,** THEN **FOLLOW** YOUR **FIRST FEELING.** EITHER **CLIMB** A **TREE** OR **PULL OFF** YOUR **SHIRT** AND **WAVE** IT IN A CIRCLE OVER YOUR **HEAD** AND **YELL, HOO-HOO-HOO-HOO!** REAL **LOUD!**

A BEAR DOESN'T LIKE LOUD NOISES. SO IF A BEAR IS IN YOUR CAMP, BANG A **METAL POT** WITH A METAL SPOON,

CLANG CLANG CLANG CLANG

OORG

OR **BANG** YOUR **METAL CANTEEN** WITH A ROCK, OR **CLACK** TWO **ROCKS TOGETHER** — LOUD!

CLACK CLACK CLACK CLACK

WEAR A BELL!

DING TING

BLOW YOUR **WHISTLE**, CLAP YOUR **HANDS**, OR BARK LIKE A **JUNKYARD DOG!**

REMEMBER, DON'T EAT WHERE YOU **SLEEP**. IN THE PARKS THE ANIMALS ARE USED TO PEOPLE, SO DON'T FEED THE ANIMALS. IF YOU FEED THEM AND THEY RUN OUT OF FOOD, THEN **YOU MAY BE THE NEXT MEAL!**

24

TELLING TIME WITH YOUR HANDS

GOOD MORNING!

HORIZON LINE

ONE HOUR
45 MINUTES
30 MINUTES
15 MINUTES

EACH **FINGER** COUNTS **15 MINUTES.**
4 FINGERS, OR ONE **HAND,** COUNTS
ONE HOUR (THUMBS DON'T COUNT).
HOLD YOUR HAND OUT IN **FRONT** OF YOU
WITH YOUR **LITTLE FINGER** ON **TOP**
OF THE **HORIZON** LINE. NOW PUT ONE
HAND ON TOP OF THE **OTHER,** UNTIL
YOU REACH THE **BOTTOM** OF THE **SUN.**

BEFORE NOON,
TWO HANDS ABOVE
HORIZON IS 8 AM.

SUN AT TOP
IS 12 NOON.

6 AM IS SUNUP.

AM
HORIZON
PM

6 HANDS FROM
HORIZON TO NOON
AND
6 HANDS FROM
NOON TO SUNDOWN.

25

DOOLEY MAKES A **LEAN-TO HOUSE** WITH A BED OF **DRY GRASS** OR **LEAVES.** FIRST, HE FINDS A **FORKED TREE IN THE WOODS** AND **BELOW A HILLTOP.** THEN HE CLEARS THE GROUND UNDER THE TREE. MAKE SURE YOU'RE **NOT** ON AN **ANT HILL!**

FORKED TREE ➤

A BROOM OF PINE TREE ↓

DITCH

SHARP ROCK ←

DOOLEY MAKES IT NICE—HE'S THERE FOR THE NIGHT AND HE'S GOING TO SLEEP ON THAT GROUND. NEXT, WITH A **SHARP ROCK,** HE DIGS A **DITCH ONE HAND WIDE** AND **4 FINGERS DEEP,** ALL AROUND WHERE HE IS GOING TO SLEEP...

SO THAT THE RAIN WATER (IT RAINS A LOT
IN THE HIGH COUNTRY) WILL RUN **INTO**
THE DITCH AND **AWAY** FROM HIM, AND
HE'LL STAY **DRY.** NEXT, USING A SHARP
ROCK, DŌŌLEY CUTS A LONG POLE
AS **THICK** AS HIS **ARM** AND **TWICE** AS **LONG**
AS **HE IS** AND PUTS IT **IN THE FORK** OF THE
TREE ... DŌŌLEY SCOOPS THE EARTH FROM
THE DITCH AND MAKES HIS BED.

THEN DŌŌLEY PILES ON SOME **DRY GRASS**
OR PINE NEEDLES **TWO HANDS HIGH** TO SLEEP ON.

NEXT DOOLEY TAKES THE **LONG POLE** HE LEANED IN THE FORK OF THE TREE AND SETS IT OVER HIS BED. THEN DOOLEY GATHERS **STICKS** AND **BRUSH**. HE LEANS THE **THICK** STICKS **AGAINST THE LONG POLE** ON EACH SIDE—LIKE THIS ⇒ ←POLE THEN HE WEAVES SOME **THIN** STICKS IN AND OUT **LONGWAYS THRU THE THICK STICKS.**

LONG POLE

WEAVE → STICKS

NOW DOOLEY PILES ON **ALL** THE **BRUSH** AND **LEAVES** HE CAN FIND AND HE ADDS **MORE STICKS** OVER THEM, SO THE WIND **DOESN'T BLOW** THEM **AWAY** WHILE HE'S SLEEPING.

28

DOOLEY USES MORE STICKS AND
BRUSH TO **CLOSE OFF** HIS DOORWAY.

HOOT HOOT
HOOT **HOOT** HOOT
HOOT HOOT
HOOT

SCREAACKCA
SCREEACKCCcHH
SCREACH
SCREEE

CHICKA
CHICKA
CHICKA
CHICKA

BOOM

CRRRK·K

WILLY DID IT

GOOD NIGHT, DOOLEY!
WHAT? OF COURSE THERE'S NO T V!
GO TO SLEEP! ZZZZZZZZ
ZZZHUH? AND DON'T BE AFRAID!
THIS LEAN-TO TAKES A WHILE TO
BUILD — SO YOU NEED TO START   CHICKA
                                CHICKA
                                CHICKA
5 HANDS BEFORE SUNDOWN.
IF YOU HEAR ANY STRANGE NOISES,
JUST ROLL OVER AND GO TO SLEEP.

29

"THE CAR IS **STUCK** IN SOFT **SAND!**"
SAYS TINA'S DAD, "AND IT'S REALLY HOT
AT NOON IN THE **DESERT,** AND I DON'T
HAVE A SHOVEL, AND WE'RE OUT OF
DRINKING WATER**!!**"

"LET'S CRAWL **UNDER THE CAR** FOR
SHADE AND TO KEEP **COOL,**"HE SAYS.
JUST BEFORE THEY DO, TINA'S DAD TAKES
OFF A **HUBCAP** ⊙. HE WAITS UNTIL THE
MOTOR **COOLS DOWN** AND THEN
SLOWLY OPENS THE RADIATOR
DRAIN PLUG.
IT'S AT THE **BOTTOM** OF THE RADIATOR.

DON'T DRINK THE RADIATOR WATER AND DON'T BREATHE ITS VAPORS— IT'S GOT CHEMICALS IN IT! TINA'S DAD FILLS THE HUBCAP. IT BECOMES A BOWL OF YUCKY WATER WHICH YOU CAN USE TO COOL OFF. TAKE OFF YOUR SHIRT AND DIP IT IN THE WATER, THEN PUT ON YOUR WET SHIRT. USE THE WATER TO COOL OFF YOUR WHOLE BODY FAST!

HERE

AND HERE ON YOUR LEGS

TINA AND DAD STAY COOL UNDER THE STUCK CAR AND PLAY A GAME CALLED LISTEN FOR A MOTOR AND ANOTHER GAME CALLED WHAT KIND OF BUG IS THAT? FUN!

WHEN THE SUN IS TWO HANDS BEFORE SUNSET ... TINA AND HER DAD CRAWL OUT

FROM UNDER THE STUCK CAR AND FOLLOW THE TIRE TRACKS OF THEIR CAR BACK TO THE MAIN ROAD AND HELP. JUST BEFORE IT GROWS DARK, TINA WALKS UP A SMALL HILL SO SHE CAN SEE BETTER, AND SHE LŌŌKS FOR LIGHTS FROM CARS AND BUILDINGS.

YOU CAN SEE A LONG WAYS IN THE DESERT. TINA AND HER DAD WALK TOWARD THE LIGHTS—

TINA'S THIRSTY! DAD SEES A BARREL CACTUS. DAD KNOWS IT'S A **PROTECTED PLANT** BUT THIS CACTUS COULD **SAVE THEIR LIVES!** BARREL CACTUS HAS THIS KIND OF A NEEDLE.

PINK OR RED NEEDLE

IT LOOKS LIKE A **FISH HOOK.**

BUT DON'T MISTAKE IT FOR A YOUNG SAGUARO (THAT'S SAW-WAH-ROW). THIS IS A SAGUARO NEEDLE →

WHITE

DON'T EVER HURT A SAGUARO!

AN OLD SAGUARO →

SAGUAROS **CAN'T HELP** THIRSTY *PEOPLE*

A BABY SAGUARO

A BARREL CACTUS

Willy DID IT

TINA'S DAD TRIES TO CUT INTO THE BARREL CACTUS WITH HIS POCKET KNIFE, BUT HE CAN'T CUT PAST THE SPRINGY NEEDLES. SO DAD PICKS UP A **BIG ROCK** AND THROWS IT AT THE BARREL CACTUS —WITH **GOOD THOUGHTS** FOR THE LITTLE CACTUS. IT MAY **SAVE THEIR LIVES!** THE ROCK BASHES AWAY THE NEEDLES AND THE OUTSIDE GREEN SKIN, SO DAD AND TINA CAN GET TO THE **WHITE MEAT PULP INSIDE.** IT'S A LOT LIKE AN APPLE INSIDE THE BARREL CACTUS. NOW DAD TAKES HIS

POCKET KNIFE AND **CUTS** OUT **PIECES** OF THE WHITE MEAT PULP AND GIVES A PIECE TO TINA...

TINA **CHEWS** A PIECE AND THEN **SPITS IT OUT!** TINA GETS THE JUICE FROM THE CACTUS PULP, THEN TRIES **ANOTHER WAY.** TINA TAKES A **BIG** PIECE OF THE BARREL CACTUS PULP AND **SQUEEZES** IT IN HER HAND, THEN **POINTS HER THUMB** AT HER MOUTH AND **DRINKS!** THE PULP JUICE RUNS DOWN TINA'S THUMB.

It's NOT THE BEST TASTE, BUT IT'S WET.

GLUG, GLUG, GLUG

How To Breathe

A Coyote hangs out his tongue and sucks air in and out. All of the blood in the Coyote's body goes thru his tongue. This cools him off. Try this Coyote trick on a hot day. Make your mouth round and curl your tongue

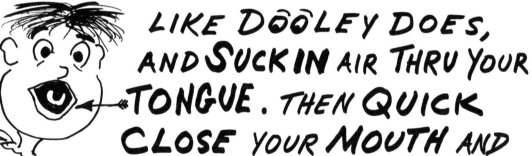

CACTUS STICKERS

like Dooley does, and suck in air thru your tongue. Then quick close your mouth and breathe out thru your nose. Do it easy. Then do it again— suck air in over your tongue, then quick close your mouth and breathe out thru your nose... Keep doing this until your tongue's cold. This will cool you off.

DOOLEY IN THE DESERT

TO KEEP HIS **MOUTH WET** WHEN HE **DOESN'T HAVE ANY WATER** AND HIS TONGUE IS DRY, DOOLEY SUCKS ON A PEBBLE **THIS SIZE** →  IT CAN BE **ANY** SHAPE JUST SO IT'S **SMOOTH**...

'CAUSE ROUGH EDGES COULD CUT YOUR MOUTH. **WIPE IT OFF** BEFORE YOU PUT IT IN YOUR MOUTH, AND DON'T FORGET TO **SPIT IT OUT** AFTER A WHILE ...

AHHH

Willy DID IT

NO, **DOOLEY, NOT** THIS SIZE!

TINA IS LOST IN THE DESERT
WITH A **BURNY SUNBURN**...

TINA LOOKS AND FINDS A **STICK** A **FOOT** long

AND AS **BIG AROUND AS HER THUMB**. SHE
PUTS A POINT ON ONE END WITH A
SHARP STONE. THEN TINA LOOKS
AND SEES A **PRICKLY PEAR**
CACTUS. TINA SENDS SOME
GOOD THOUGHTS TO THE
LITTLE CACTUS, FOR IT
WILL **COOL** AND
PROTECT HER **SKIN.** TINA **POKES**
THE STICK **INTO A PAD**
BETWEEN THE **NEEDLES**...
AND GETS THE CACTUS JUICE ON THE STICK.
SHE **WIPES OFF** THE JUICE WITH HER
FINGERS . . .

• • • AND THEN **RUBS** THE **JUICE** ON HER **FACE**, **NECK**, **EARS**, **LIPS**, **ARMS**, AND **NOSE**. TINA KEEPS POKING THE STICK **BACK INTO** THE **SAME PLACE** IN THE CACTUS PAD TO GET **MORE** OF THE JUICE. TINA KNOWS THAT THIS WAY THE LITTLE CACTUS PAD WILL **HEAL** BACK UP AFTER IT HAS SAVED HER SKIN FROM THE HOT SUN.

WATER IN THE DESERT

TINA CLIMBS A **LOW HILL** JUST AT **SUNSET** AND LOOKS AROUND! THE SUN SHINES OFF A **POOL** OF WATER LIKE A **MIRROR**. THE POOL OF WATER IS TOO FAR AWAY FOR TINA TO WALK TO BEFORE IT GETS DARK, SO TINA DRAWS AN **ARROW ON** THE GROUND POINTING **RIGHT TOWARD THE** POOL OF **WATER.**

THEN SHE DRAWS **ANOTHER LINE** TO PUT HER **TOES** ON, SO

SHE CAN HIKE DOWN AND **FIND THE** POOL OF **WATER IN THE MORNING.**

40

WHILE IT'S STILL LIGHT, TINA LOOKS FOR A **HILL**, A **ROCK**, OR A **BIG TREE** AROUND THE SPOT WHERE SHE SEES THE POOL OF WATER.

THE NEXT MORNING, TINA WAKES UP AND CLIMBS THE **SAME** HILL. SHE PUTS HER **TOES** ON THE **LINE** SHE DREW AND LOOKS TO WHERE HER **ARROW'S** POINTING. IN THE MORNING SUNLIGHT, TINA CAN'T SEE THE POOL OF WATER. BUT SHE REMEMBERS WHAT WAS **AROUND** IT—AND HIKES ON DOWN TO FIND IT.

THE WATER TREES

TINA SEES THE SUMMER SNOW OF THE DESERT GO PAST HER ON THE WIND. THESE ARE COTTON BALLS FROM THE COTTON WOOD TREES — THEY ARE A SIGN OF A TREE THAT **LOVES WATER**. THE COTTONWOOD LEAF LOOKS LIKE THIS.

ARIZONA BUMPUR STICKUR

THE LEAF IS A **BRIGHT SILVERY GREEN**. TINA CLIMBS A LOW HILL IN THE DESERT AND LOOKS AROUND FOR THE **BRIGHTEST GREEN** TREES. TINA HIKES OVER TO THEM AND FINDS A POOL OF WATER! IF YOU **DON'T** FIND WATER **ON TOP** OF THE GROUND, THEN YOU WILL HAVE TO **DIG DOWN** TO FIND IT.

IN THE DESERT, TINA FINDS **WATER** UNDER A **COTTONWOOD TREE**.

43

DOOLEY FINDS A POND OF YUCKY LOOKING WATER WITH GREEN MOSS AND POLLYWOGS

ARRRGH

SAND FILTER ONE FOOT

ONE FOOT

YUCKY WATER

SIDE VIEW

DOOLEY'S HOLE

SO DOOLEY DIGS A HOLE **ONE FOOT** AWAY IN THE SAND. THE SAND BETWEEN THE YUCKY WATER AND DOOLEY'S HOLE ACTS AS A **FILTER**, AND THE WATER SEEPS SLOWLY INTO DOOLEY'S HOLE. IF THE YUCKY WATER HOLE HAS **NO POLLYWOGS** OR **TINY FISH** IN IT, OR THERE ARE **DEAD ANIMAL BONES** NEAR IT, THEN THAT IS **BAD WATER**. DON'T DRINK IT! USE IT LIKE **RADIATOR WATER** TO KEEP YOU COOL. SEE PAGE **31.**

HERE COME THE MOSQUITOES

NEEEEEAA NEEEEE NEEEE

NEEEEEA

WHAT DOES DOOLEY DO?
HE PUTS **MUD** ON HIS **FACE** AND **HANDS**,
WHEREVER THE MOSQUITOES CAN GET TO,
HANDS, ARMS, EARS, NECK . . .

EEEEKK

HA!
HA!

THE MOSQUITOES CAN'T GET THEIR
NEEDLE NOSES THRU THE **MUD**. THE MUD
WASHES OFF. IT SURE BEATS SCRATCHING
MOSQUITO BITES. IT WORKS FOR
NO-SEE-UMS TOO! WHAT BIT ME?
I NO-SEE-UM! CHEROKEES USED TO PUT
MUD ON SKEETER BITES AND STINGS.

45

EMERGENCY FOOD

DOOLEY LOOKS AT ALL THE **LEAVES** AND **BERRIES** AND **FLOWERS** AND **TREES**.

"CAN I EAT THEM?" HE ASKS. **TO FIND OUT,** HERE'S AN OLD **CHEROKEE** WAY OF TESTING THE WILD PLANTS, SO YOU **DON'T GET SICK** OR WORSE **CROAK!** HERE ARE **5 STEPS** TO **TEST** A **WILD PLANT** SO IT DOES **NOT POISON** YOU:

① MAKE SURE THERE'S **ENOUGH** LEAVES, BERRIES, FLOWERS, FRUIT, OR INSIDE-TREE BARK TO **MAKE A MEAL** ... **LOOK!**

IF YOU SEE THIS ↑ — THEN DON'T EAT THIS ↑

2 CRUSH A LEAF OR BERRY OR FRUIT IN YOUR FINGERS AND SMELL IT. DOES THE LEAF OR FRUIT SMELL LIKE ANYTHING YOU WANT TO EAT? IF NOT, GO LOOK FOR ANOTHER PLANT AND START OVER.

3 IT SMELLS YUMMY! OKAY, NOW TAKE A SMALL PIECE THIS BIG ➤➤ ▦ . RUB IT ON YOUR GUMS 👄 ON ONE LITTLE SPOT × AND CHEW IT ON THE TIPS OF YOUR FRONT TEETH. NOW SPIT IT OUT AND DON'T SWALLOW YOUR SALIVA! WAIT 20 MINUTES.

DOES YOUR TONGUE OR GUMS BURN? DO YOU FEEL DIZZY? IF YOU DON'T LIKE THE TASTE OR YOU FEEL DIZZY, THEN SPIT OUT ALL OF YOUR SALIVA! GO FIND ANOTHER PLANT AND START ALL OVER. IF YOU LIKED IT, THEN GO TO STEP 4.

OKAY

TO STEP 4

OKAY

WILLY DID IT

4) TAKE **ANOTHER** LITTLE PIECE OF THE FRUIT OR LEAF — **THIS BIG** →. CHEW IT WITH YOUR **FRONT TEETH**, THEN **SPIT IT OUT**. NOW **SWALLOW** A **LITTLE BIT** OF YOUR **SALIVA** AND **WAIT ANOTHER 20 MINUTES!** **ASK** YOURSELF HOW YOU **FEEL**. IF YOU FEEL **DIZZY** OR **SICK**, **FORGET** THAT PLANT. GO FIND **ANOTHER** AND **START OVER**.

IF YOU FEEL **OKAY**, THEN GO TO STEP...

5) TAKE ANOTHER PIECE **THIS BIG** →. CHEW IT UP AND **SWALLOW IT**. NOW **WAIT ONE HOUR**... AND IF YOU **STILL** FEEL OKAY **AFTER THE ONE HOUR IS UP**, THEN GO AHEAD AND EAT **SOME MORE**. IF **NOT**, FIND **ANOTHER** PLANT AND GO **BACK** TO STEP① ON PAGE **46**.

SURE YOU'RE HUNGRY, BUT A LOT OF KIDS HAVE CROAKED BY EATING THE WRONG PLANT! SO DON'T TAKE

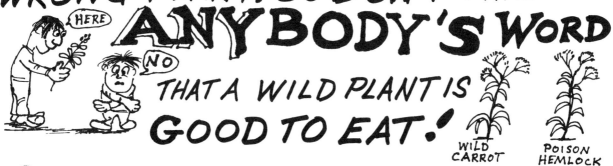

HERE

NO

ANYBODY'S WORD THAT A WILD PLANT IS **GOOD TO EAT!**

WILD CARROT

POISON HEMLOCK

SHOW THEM HOW TO DO THIS **5-STEP TEST.** THAT'S WHY YOU WANT TO **FIRST** MAKE SURE THERE'S **PLENTY** TO **EAT,** 'CAUSE YOU'VE GOT TO **WAIT** ONE HOUR AND **40 MINUTES** — **7 FINGERS** HAND TIME, AND EVEN **LONGER** IF YOU NEED **ANOTHER** PLANT. **EAT SLOW** AND **JUST ENOUGH TO FILL YOU UP.** WILD FOOD IS **NOT** FAST FOOD, A **LITTLE** GOES A **LONG** WAY. **ENJOY!**

FLIP

49

MORE EMERGENCY FOOD

TINA GETS HUNGRY WHILE SHE'S **LOST**. SHE KNOWS YOU CAN EAT THE INSIDE BARK OF **MOST** TREES, BUT SOME CAN MAKE YOU SICK, SO TINA USES THE 5-STEP TEST ON PAGE **46**.

THE CHEROKEES HAVE RECIPES TO MAKE MEALS FROM TREE BARK, SO LET'S TAKE A LŌŌK AT A TREE...

 **TREE LOOKS LIKE THIS:**

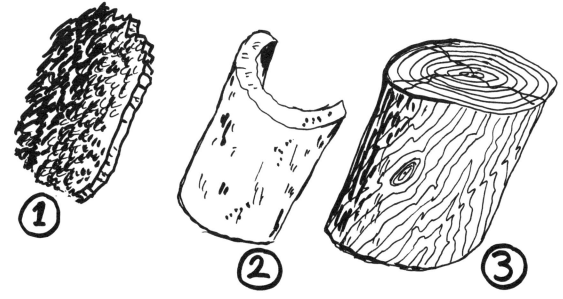

① THE OUTSIDE BARK

② THE INSIDE BARK

③ THE WOOD

WHICH ONE CAN YOU **EAT**?

✓ CHECK ①, ②, OR ③

IF YOU CHECKED ②,
   YOU'LL **MAKE IT**!

TINA USES A **SHARP STONE** TO PEEL OFF THE **OUTSIDE** BARK. TAKING BARK **HURTS** THE TREE, SO SHE TAKES ONLY A SMALL PIECE **THIS BIG** →

FROM **JUST ONE BRANCH**.

TINA DOES THE **5-STEP TEST** ON IT, SEE PAGE 46, TO **MAKE SURE** THE BARK IS **OKAY TO EAT**...

IF IT'S **OKAY**, TINA **CHOPS** OR **SCRAPES** OFF THE **OUTSIDE** BARK SO SHE CAN GET **ENOUGH INSIDE BARK** TO MAKE A **MEAL**.

THEN TINA **PEELS OFF THE INSIDE BARK.** THE BARK IS TOUGH AND CHEWY, SO TINA LAYS IT ON A **FLAT** ROCK AND **POUNDS** IT WITH A **ROUND** ROCK TO MAKE THE BARK **EASIER** TO EAT. IF TINA HAS A **FIRE,** SHE CAN EVEN **COOK** THE BARK. **FIRST,** SHE **POUNDS** IT TO MAKE IT **REAL SOFT.**

YUMMY PIECE OF INNER TREE BARK→

ROUND ←ROCK

I'M LEAVING

FLAT ROCK

NEXT, TINA ADDS A LITTLE **WATER** AND **MOOSHES** IT TOGETHER. THEN SHE PUTS THE MOOSHED BARK ON A **LARGE FLAT** ROCK AND **BAKES** IT **NEAR** THE FIRE LIKE **BREAD.** YUM!

GOING POTTY

A CAT DIGS A HOLE AND **BURIES** HIS DOO-DOO...

A DOG GOES WEE-WEE IN THE BUSHES...

HOW DOES DOOLEY DOO-DOO?

DOOLEY DIGS A HOLE, USING A STICK OR A SHARP ROCK. **AFTER** HE GOES POTTY, HE **COVERS** HIS DOO-DOO AND HIS TOILET PAPER WITH **EARTH** AND THEN PUTS A **BIG ROCK** ON TOP, SO **NO ANIMAL** CAN **DIG** IT **UP**! THAT WAY, DOOLEY LEAVES THE OUTDOORS **NEAT** AND **CLEAN.**

THINGS TO WATCH

TOUCHING THESE **3-LEAVES** CAN GIVE YOU THE **ITCHY-SCRATCHIES**.

GREEN → ←POISON IVY

POISON → OAK

GREEN TO RED TO YELLOW TO BROWN

DON'T SCRATCH, DOOLEY, DO WHAT THE CHEROKEES DO! WASH WITH WATER AND PUT **GOOEY** MUD ON THE **ITCH**.

BEFORE TINA PUTS HER **SHOES** ON, SHE **SHAKES OUT** ANY **CRAWLY CRITTERS AWAY** FROM HER.

IN THE DESERT, DOOLEY USES A **STICK** TO TURN OVER A ROCK **BEFORE** HE **PICKS** IT **UP**. **CRAWLY CRITTERS** LIVE **UNDER ROCKS**.

DOOLEY AND TINA SEE A SNAKE

"I WONDER IF IT'S A POISON SNAKE?" HE ASKS. TINA SAYS, "I KNOW HOW TO TELL, 'CAUSE CRAWLERS AND BUGS HAVE A COLOR CODE. HERE'S AN OLD CHEROKEE RHYME:

RED TOUCH YELLOW, HIM DEADLY FELLA!

RED TOUCH BLACK HIM BAD FELLA!

YELLOW TOUCH BLACK, FRIEND OF JACK!"
IF YOU GET BIT, REMEMBER THE COLORS SO YOU CAN TELL SOMEONE.

I GOT BIT BY A RED AND BLACK SPIDER!

OKAY!

56

AFRICAN **KILLER BEES**

ARE A WHOLE LOT **MEANER** THAN OUR REGULAR, HOME-GROWN BEES.

THEY LIKE THE DARK COLORS, SO WEAR WHITE OR LIGHT-COLORED SHIRT OR CAP WHEN IN WILD BEE COUNTRY. IF A BEE COMES AROUND, YOU STAND VERY STILL AND DON'T SWAT AT HIM. IF YOU SWAT AT HIM OR HURT HIM, HE WILL GIVE A HIGH PITCH BUZZZZZZZZZZZZZZZZZZZZZZ AND THE WHOLE BEE TRIBE WILL COME TO HELP HIM!

WHASSA MATTA?

HE HIT ME!

THEN IT'S BEST TO RUN JUMP IN ANY CREEK OR WATER. COVER UP WITH MUD—LOTS OF IT! POUR YOUR CANTEEN ON THE EARTH TO MAKE MUD QUICK!

57

FIRE

IF YOU ARE **LOST** AND IT LOOKS LIKE YOU'RE GOING TO BE IN THE **WOODS** FOR THE **NIGHT**, A **FIRE** WILL KEEP YOU **WARM**, **COOK** YOUR **FOOD**, AND **HELP PEOPLE** WHO ARE LOOKING FOR YOU TO **FIND** YOU.

FIRST, **CLEAR** A **BIG AREA** OF ALL **GRASS** AND **BRUSH** SO THAT YOU **DON'T BURN DOWN** THE **WOODS** OR **FOREST**. A FIRE CAN BE A REAL FRIEND TO A COLD LOST KID. SO LET'S BUILD A **FRIENDLY** FIRE.

DOOLEY HAS NOTHING TO START A FIRE WITH, SO HE MAKES A **FIRE** WITH **STICKS** THE OLD **CHEROKEE WAY**. DOOLEY USES HIS **SHOESTRING** INSTEAD OF A CORD MADE FROM PLANTS.

TO **MAKE** A **FIRE**, THE **FIRST** THING
DOOLEY LOOKS FOR IS A BRANCH
WITH A **BOW** IN IT **AS LONG** AS HIS **ARM**
AND **AS BIG AROUND AS** HIS **THUMB.**

BOW

DOOLEY SENDS SOME **GOOD THOUGHTS**
TO THE **TREE** AS HE CUTS OFF THE **BRANCH,**
USING A **SHARP STONE.** THEN HE **NOTCHES**
THE BOW **HERE** AND **HERE.**

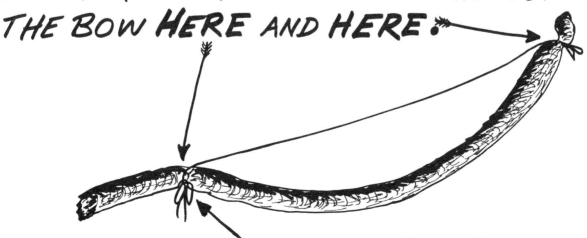

THEN DOOLEY **TIES** HIS **SHOELACE** TO IT.

THE NEXT THING DOOLEY NEEDS IS A DRY STRAIGHT STICK ONE FOOT LONG AND AS BIG AROUND AS HIS THUMB. HE SHARPENS ONE END TO A POINT AND HE ROUNDS OFF THE OTHER END SO IT LOOKS LIKE THIS ➤ A DRILL!

NEXT, DOOLEY LOOKS AROUND FOR A DRY DEAD BRANCH OF ALMOST SOFT WOOD AND HE DOES THIS TO IT!

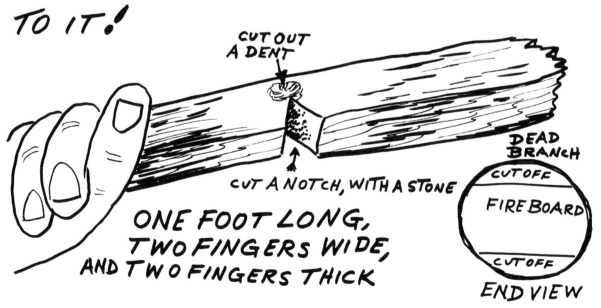

CUT OUT A DENT

CUT A NOTCH, WITH A STONE

DEAD BRANCH
CUT OFF
FIRE BOARD
CUT OFF
END VIEW

ONE FOOT LONG, TWO FINGERS WIDE, AND TWO FINGERS THICK

THIS IS DOOLEY'S FIRE BOARD!

NEXT, DŌŌLEY LOOKS AROUND FOR A PIECE OF **WOOD** OR A **STONE** WITH A **DENT** IN IT IN THE MIDDLE, OR HE PUTS A DENT IN IT WITH A **POINTED STONE.**

DENT

THIS **HAND BLOCK** PROTECTS DOOLEY'S HAND.
NOW LŌŌK AT DOOLEY'S **FIRE-MAKING TOOLS:**

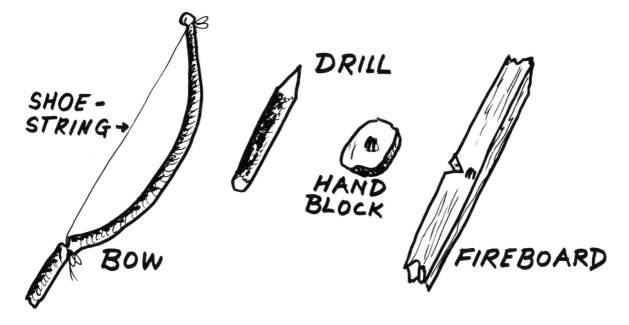

SHOE-STRING →

DRILL

HAND BLOCK

BOW

FIREBOARD

NOW WHAT **ELSE** DOES DOOLEY NEED?

NOW DOOLEY LOOKS AROUND FOR *TINDER* TO START A FIRE...

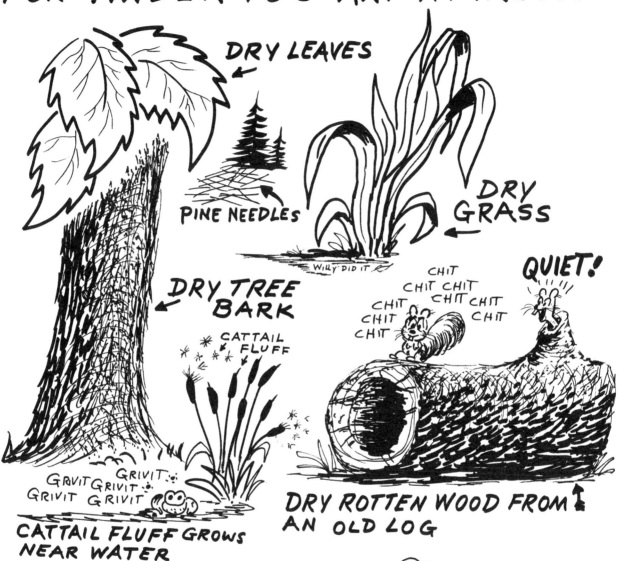

DRY LEAVES

PINE NEEDLES

DRY GRASS

WILLY DID IT

DRY TREE BARK

CATTAIL FLUFF

CHIT CHIT CHIT CHIT CHIT CHIT CHIT CHIT CHIT CHIT

QUIET!

GRIVIT GRIVIT GRIVIT GRIVIT GRIVIT

DRY ROTTEN WOOD FROM AN OLD LOG

CATTAIL FLUFF GROWS NEAR WATER

IF IT LOOKS LIKE *RAIN*, THEN HE GATHERS HIS *DRY TINDER* EARLY AND PUTS IT IN HIS POCKET OR PACK, SO HE CAN *START A FIRE* AFTER THE RAIN IS OVER.

Now Dooley CRUSHES up the dry tinder with his HANDS until it's ALMOST A POWDER. He has enough to make it the size of A SOFT BALL ⚾.

Next, Dooley and Tina look around for FIREWOOD. They gather up OLD DRY wood and sticks from the GROUND, not from LIVING trees—THAT wood is WET inside and WON'T burn EASY.

If it starts to rain, Dooley COVERS his dry firewood with LOTS of LEAVES or PINE NEEDLES to keep it DRY. After a rain, he breaks off FINGER-LONG TIPS of tree branches. They have a WAXY coating and can HELP Dooley START A FIRE, 'cause the water HASN'T made 'em soggy.

DOOLEY SETS SOME **ROCKS** IN A **2-FOOT** CIRCLE IN THE **MIDDLE** OF HIS **CLEARED GROUND.** THEN HE PUTS DOWN **2 HANDFULS** OF DRY GRASS, DRY **LEAVES, TINDER WOOD,** OR **PINE NEEDLES.** THEN HE **PUSHES 3 PENCIL-SIZE** STICKS INTO THE GROUND AROUND THE LEAVES TO BUILD A STICK **TEEPEE.**

NOW HE **LEANS MORE STICKS** ONTO THESE 3, SO HIS FIRE **WON'T FALL OVER** AND SO IT'LL **BURN FAST** AND **EASY.** DOOLEY TAKES SOME **LONG,** DEAD BRANCHES AND **BREAKS** 'EM UP **LIKE THIS** FOR **FIRE WOOD.**

DEAD BRANCH

THROW

HIT HERE

BIG ROCK

ROCK FASTER THAN AN AX!

DOOLEY GETS HIS **FIRE-MAKING TOOLS**-SEE PAGE **61**. FIRST, HE MAKES HIS TINDER INTO A **TIGHT BALL** WITH HIS HANDS ~ SQUEEZE. THEN HE LAYS IT ON THE GROUND, **OUTSIDE** HIS ROCK CIRCLE.

← FIREWOOD

SECOND TINDER

LIZARD ←

FIRE BOARD →

FIRST TINDER SOFTBALL SIZE

NEXT, HE PUTS HIS **FIRE BOARD** WITH THE NOTCH ON **TOP** OF THE SOFTBALL-SIZE TINDER. THEN DOOLEY PICKS UP HIS **BOW** AND **DRILL**. HE HOLDS THE DRILL WITH THE **POINTED** END **UP**, AND GIVES THE DRILL A QUICK **WRAP** AROUND THE BOWSTRING SHOELACE.

TWANG TIGHT!

← LOOP

DOOLEY NEXT HOLDS THE
HAND BLOCK  WITH ONE HAND AND
BOW AND DRILL TIGHTLY WITH
HIS OTHER HAND, SO THE DRILL
DOESN'T FLIP OUT. HE THEN PUTS
ONE FOOT ON TOP OF THE FIRE BOARD,
ONE FINGER AWAY FROM THE NOTCH.

←TINDER

DOOLEY KNEELS DOWN ON
ONE KNEE. HE PUTS THE DENT
OF THE HAND BLOCK ON TOP OF THE
POINTED END OF THE DRILL–AND
FITS THE ROUND END OF THE DRILL
INTO THE DENT AT THE END OF THE
NOTCH IN THE FIRE BOARD.

LIKE THIS

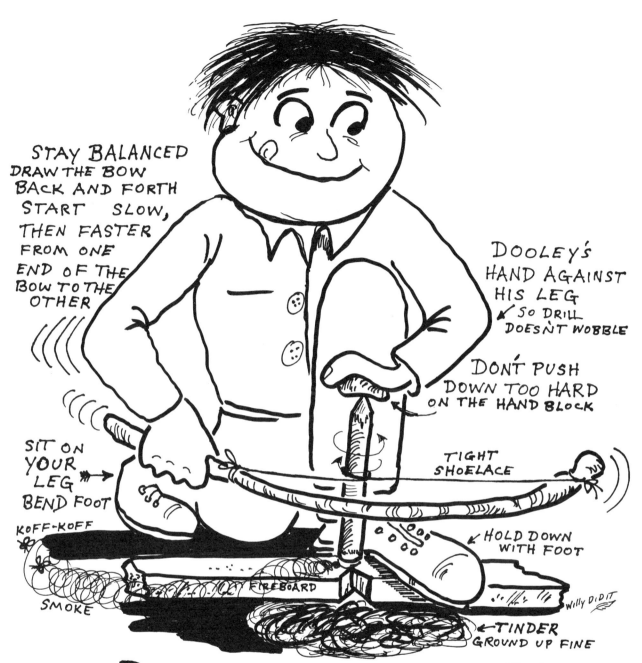

DOOLEY MOVES THE BOW *BACK* AND *FORTH FAST,* UNTIL HE MAKES SMOKE AND A LITTLE *RED HOT COAL* SHOWS UP IN THE *NOTCH* . . .

67

DOOLEY BLOWS *STEADY ON THE* RED HOT LITTLE COAL . . .

WHOoo

TINDER

THEN HE TAKES A *TOOTHPICK-SIZE* TWIG AND **POKES** THE COAL *INTO THE* TINDER. HE CUPS HIS HANDS *AROUND* THE TINDER AND **KEEPS ON** BLOWING UNTIL **FIRE STARTS.** DOOLEY SETS *THE* **BURNING** TINDER ON THE **SECOND** TINDER WAITING BY *THE* **STICK TEEPEE.**

I'M WAITING

SECOND TINDER

FIRST TINDER

WHOO

FIREWOOD GOES ON LAST

By **SUNDOWN**, DOOLEY AND TINA HAVE A **CAMPFIRE** TO KEEP **WARM**.

↑ENOUGH TO LAST THE NIGHT.

MAKE A SMALL FIRE AND SIT CLOSE.

DOOLEY WAS SMART TO LOOK FOR HIS **FIRE-MAKING** TOOLS **5 HANDS BEFORE SUNSET** – 'CAUSE AFTER IT GETS DARK, YOU MIGHT PICK UP A **SNAKE** INSTEAD OF A STICK.

IF DOOLEY AND TINA CAN ONLY FIND **WET** WOOD, THEY PUT IT **AROUND** THEIR FIRE TO **DRY** IT OUT, LIKE THIS...

I'M WET TOO!

HAVE PLENTY OF WOOD!

AS IT DRIES, THEY GIVE IT TO THE FIRE TO **KEEP IT GOING**.

TINA SHOWS DOOLEY A WAY TO
MAKE FIRE WITHOUT A BOW

TINA KNOWS HOW TO MAKE A FIRE WHEN SHE **HASN'T ANY** SHOESTRINGS OR CORD, AND THERE ARE **NO PLANTS** AROUND TO MAKE A CORD FROM AND **NO TREES** TO GIVE HER A BOW. THIS WAY CAN TAKE A **LITTLE LONGER.**

TINA LOOKS FOR A **DRY STICK** AS LONG AS HER **ARM AND HAND** AND **REAL STRAIGHT**, AND AS BIG AROUND AS HER **LITTLE FINGER.** SHE **ROUNDS** OFF **ONE END** OF THE STICK ON A ROUGH ROCK. SHE BORROWS DOOLEY'S **FIRE BOARD** AND PUTS A **NEW NOTCH** IN IT, AND CUTS A LITTLE DENT **BEHIND** THE NOTCH LIKE DOOLEY DID ON **PAGE 60** . . .

HERE'S HOW TINA **STARTS** HER FIRE. FIRST, SHE SITS ON A LOG OR ROCK. SHE PUTS HER **TINDER**  DOWN, THE SIZE OF A **SOFTBALL**, AND LAYS THE FIRE BOARD **ON TOP** OF IT. THEN TINA **SPITS** ON HER **PALMS** AND SHE **TWIRLS** HER STICK, KEEPING HER HANDS **FLAT** AND **MOVING** THEM **FAST BACK** AND **FORTH**, UNTIL A **RED HOT** COAL SHOWS UP IN THE **NOTCH!**

THEN TINA DOES THE SAME THING DOOLEY DID ON **PAGE 68.**

A LITTLE LATER, LITTLE BROTHER **TATER** SHOWS UP!

TINA AND DOOLEY LOOK AT EACH OTHER. IT'S TOUGH TO BE LOST, BUT NOW THEY HAVE THEIR LITTLE BROTHER TO **HELP OUT,** SO HERE'S WHAT TINA AND DOOLEY DO...

72

DOOLEY MAKES UP A LITTLE MUD, THIS MUCH ➡ [scribble] AND PUTS IT ON TATER'S BEE STING, WHILE TINA MAKES A PLACE FOR TATER TO SIT BY THE FIRE TO KEEP WARM.

TINA USES AN OLD CHEROKEE WAY TO STOP THE PAIN IN TATER'S KNEE. TINA PUTS TWO FINGERS ON TATER'S KNEE WHERE THE PAIN IS AND THEN, WITH HER OTHER HAND, SHE PUTS TWO FINGERS ON THE STRONG PULSE DRUMBEAT ON TATER'S THROAT, JUST UNDER HIS JAWBONE ...

WHEN TINA FEELS THE **SAME STEADY DRUMBEAT** ON TATER'S HURT **KNEE** THRU HER TWO FINGERS, SHE LETS GO. THIS TAKES ABOUT AS LONG AS A THIRSTY DOG DOES TO DRINK WATER.

THE **CHEROKEES** CALL THIS **BALANCING** THE **NORTH** AND **SOUTH DRUM** OF THE **BODY**. TINA PUTS TWO FINGERS ON TATER'S **PULSE** DRUMBEAT AND, WITH HER **OTHER** HAND, SHE PUTS TWO FINGERS ON THE **PAIN** OR **HURT** ON **ANY** PART OF TATER'S BODY— THIS WORKS FOR **ALL KINDS** OF PAIN WHEN YOU **CAN'T GET TO** A **DOCTOR**.

TINA SHOWS TATER HOW TO **SLEEP ON A CAMPFIRE** TO KEEP WARM THRU THE **NIGHT.** FIRST, SHE FINDS A **SHARP ROCK**, THEN **5 FEET** AWAY FROM THE CAMPFIRE, SHE **SCRAPES** THE EARTH AND **DIGS** A **FIRE PIT 4 FINGERS DEEP, 3 FEET LONG,** AND **2 FEET WIDE.**

FIREWOOD

SCRAPING ROCK

5 FEET

4 FINGERS DEEP

3 FEET

Willy DID IT

I'M LEAVING

TINA PILES UP THE EARTH **AROUND** THE **EDGE** OF THE PIT. NEXT, WITH A **FORKED** STICK, SHE PUTS A PIECE OF **BURNING WOOD** IN THE **MIDDLE** OF THE PIT AND ADDS **MORE FIREWOOD,** UNTIL SHE HAS **ANOTHER FIRE.**

NOW TINA, DOOLEY, AND TATER
HAVE TWO CAMPFIRES—ONE TO KEEP
THEIR FRONTS WARM AND ONE TO KEEP
THEIR BACKS WARM.

HOOTA HOOT

HOOT

WILLY DID IT

← STICK TO SPREAD COALS OUT

TINA AND DOOLEY LET THE FIRE IN THE
PIT BURN LOW.
NOW TATER IS TRULY TOTALLY TIRED,
SO TINA TAKES AN ARM-LONG STICK
AND SPREADS OUT THE COALS
EVENLY INSIDE THE PIT...

NEXT TINA POURS *EARTH* ON *ALL* THE *HOT* COALS **7** FINGERS DEEP...

... WHEN SHE'S SURE *ALL* THE COALS ARE *COVERED*, TINA *PATS* DOWN THE EARTH AND MAKES IT *SMOOTH*. NOW LITTLE TATER CAN LIE DOWN TO *SLEEP* ON HIS *WARM BED*.

OLD CHEROKEE WAYS CAN HELP YOU WHEN YOU'RE LOST.

78

TINA AND DOOLEY MAKE **SURE** THEIR **CAMPFIRE** IS **OUT** WHEN THEY LEAVE CAMP. THEY PUT EARTH ON TOP OF THE HOT COALS 4 FINGERS DEEP. IF THEY'RE CAMPED NEAR A STREAM OR A LAKE, THEY POUR **WATER** ON THE COALS, AND THEN 2 FINGERS DEEP OF EARTH ON TOP. **WHY** DO TINA AND DOOLEY DO THIS? 'CAUSE THE **WIND** CAN COME UP AND CARRY A RED HOT COAL INTO THE TREES...

...AND WE LIVE HERE!

...AND THE SMELL OF A LIVE PINE FOREST IS LOTS BETTER THAN THE SMELL OF A BURNT ONE. YEP!

FINDING NORTH

THE NIGHT SKY WILL HELP YOU TO FIND NORTH. THIS IS A DIPPER:

THERE IS ALSO A BIG DIPPER IN THE NIGHT SKY. SOMETIMES IT FACES ONE WAY, SOMETIMES ANOTHER WAY.

LOOK FOR IT! IT HAS **7** STARS.

DOOLEY FINDS THE **2** STARS ON THE END OF THE DIPPER'S CUP. HE LOOKS ALONG THEM AND THE FIRST STAR ON HIS MAKE-BELIEVE LINE IS THE NORTH STAR. IT'S NOT REAL BRIGHT.

HERE I AM!

← MAKE BELIEVE LINE

TINA FINDS NORTH

IN THE WOODS, TINA LOOKS AND SEES THE GREEN MOSS ON THE TREES. THAT SIDE IS NORTH—THE SIDE WITHOUT THE MOSS IS SOUTH.

THE SUN COMES UP IN THE EAST AND GOES DOWN IN THE WEST, SO THESE ARE THE 4 DIRECTIONS →

BEFORE LEAVING CAMP, DOOLEY AND TINA WALK A SMALL CIRCLE AROUND THEIR CAMP AND LOOK NORTH, WEST, SOUTH, AND EAST. DO WHAT TINA AND DOOLEY DO—REMEMBER WHAT YOU SEE, SO YOU CAN FIND YOUR WAY BACK!

TALKING STICKS

LONG AGO, THE CHEROKEES USED TALKING STICKS. TODAY THEY ARE CALLED DOWSING STICKS. TALKING STICKS CAN HELP YOU **FIND WATER** OR YOUR **WAY BACK** TO CAMP IF YOU'RE **LOST.** HERE'S HOW TO MAKE A PAIR FOR YOURSELF...

DŌŌLEY LŌŌKS AROUND FOR A **BUSH** THAT HAS SOME **FORKED** BRANCHES, AND HE SENDS SOME **GOOD THOUGHTS** TO THE BUSH AS HE CUTS **2** SMALL BRANCHES **WITH FORKS** SO THEY LŌŌK LIKE THIS

AS LONG AS YOUR FOOT→

THE OLD CHEROKEES NEVER GOT LOST. THEY TALKED TO EVERYTHING — TREES, ROCKS, PLANTS, ANIMALS, BIRDS, WATERS — AND THEY LIVED **HAPPY.**

OH-SEE-OH

82

DOOLEY HOLDS HIS TALKING STICKS

LIKE THIS:

THUMB ON END

HOLD 'EM LEVEL

PALMS UP FINGERS STRAIGHT

END

FORKS JOINED →

HE HOLDS THE ENDS **GENTLY**, SO THAT THE STICKS CAN MOVE BY THEMSELVES **FREELY**. DOOLEY KEEPS THE **PALMS** OF HIS HANDS **UP** AND HIS **FINGERS STRAIGHT**.

NOW DOOLEY SAYS **OUT LOUD**, "I'M LOST! CAN YOU POINT THE **WAY BACK** TO **CAMP**?" OR HE SAYS, "TINA IS LOST. CAN YOU POINT THE WAY TO **FIND HER**?" **WHATEVER** HIS QUESTION IS, THE STICKS WILL MOVE **BY THEMSELVES** LIKE THIS. AND **POINT** TO WHAT DOOLEY ASKS FOR.

DOOLEY ASKS THE STICKS TO **POINT BACK** TO **CAMP**...AND AS HE ASKS, HE SLOWLY TURNS IN A **CIRCLE**, HOLDING THEM **LEVEL**.

CIRCLE SLOW LIKE AN EAGLE

REMEMBER, KIDS, TO **FIND** YOUR **WAY BACK**, ALWAYS ASK FOR **SOMETHING** THAT'S **IN ONE PLACE**. IF YOU ASK WHERE YOUR MOM AND DAD'S CAR IS AND THEY'RE DRIVING AROUND LOOKING FOR YOU, YOU'LL **JUST** GO **IN CIRCLES**.

DOOLEY ASKS FOR ONLY ONE THING
AT A TIME. TO TEST HIS NEW STICKS,
DOOLEY LAYS HIS BELT DOWN ON THE
GROUND AND WALKS ABOUT 7 STEPS
AWAY FROM IT...

OH BOY!
OH WOW!
A BELT!

NAW!
IT'S A
FLAT SNAKE!

HOLDING HIS STICKS **LEVEL**, DOOLEY
CLOSES HIS EYES AND SAYS, "POINT TO MY
BELT," AS HE TURNS SLOWLY IN A CIRCLE.
WHEN HE FACES HIS BELT, THE STICKS SHOULD
BE POINTING AT IT.

NOW DOOLEY SAYS: "POINT THE WAY
TO OUR CAMP." IF THE STICKS POINTED
RIGHT TO DOOLEY'S BELT, THEN
WHEN HE TURNS IN A CIRCLE, THE
STICKS SHOULD POINT HIS WAY BACK
TO CAMP.

85

POCKETS AND PACKS

HERE ARE SOME THINGS TO PUT IN YOUR JACKET POCKET:

① A WHISTLE ON A STRING, FOR AROUND YOUR NECK

② A LITTLE BAG OF TRAIL MIX TO EAT

③ SOME *TOILET PAPER* IN A LITTLE SACK

④ 25 FEET OF STRING

⑤ A FOLD-UP HAT FOR RAIN OR SUN

⑥ A SMALL FLASHLIGHT ON A STRING, FOR AROUND YOUR NECK

⑦ A LITTLE NOTE PAD AND PENCIL, FOR LEAVING NOTES IF YOU GO AWAY

⑧ A PLASTIC FOLD-UP-TIGHT RAINCOAT OR A PLASTIC 30 GALLON TRASH BAG WITH HOLES CUT FOR YOUR HEAD AND ARMS

IS THIS *TOO MUCH STUFF?* THEN...

BELT PACKS
...A BELT PACK WILL HOLD MORE!

⑨ A CANTEEN FOR WATER

⑩ A WOOL PULLOVER CAP, FOR WHEN IT'S COLD

⑪ GLOVES, EITHER WOOL OR LEATHER

⑫ 6 PLASTIC VEGETABLE BAGS

⑬ A TUBE OF OUTDOOR SKIN LOTION

⑭ A LITTLE METAL MIRROR, FOR SIGNALING FOR HELP

IS THIS **STILL** TOO MUCH **STUFF**? THEN...

BACK PACKS

A SMALL BACK PACK WILL HOLD ALL YOU NEED, SO WHEN MOM OR DAD SAY LET'S GO! YOU'RE READY TO GO RIGHT AWAY!

CHEROKEE BUCKSKIN CARRY BAG

MAKE ONE OR BUY ONE

(15) A WOOL SWEATER

(16) A LEAKPROOF PLASTIC BOTTLE OF WATER, PINT OR QUART, NOT GLASS

GLASS BREAKS!

CRASH

(17) A WARM THERMAL FOLD-UP-TIGHT BLANKET

(18) A SMILE!

WAIT! DOOLEY, YOU FORGOT THE ANVIL!

ASK YOUR MOM OR DAD ABOUT POCKET KNIVES, MATCHES, AND WATER PURIFICATION TABLETS!

PARENTS: PLEASE SEE NOTE ON PAGE 95.

LITTLE TATER WANDERS AWAY FROM CAMP, AND **NOBODY SAW HIM** LEAVE! MOM PUT A **BRIGHT RED** FLUORESCENT **VEST** ON HIM, SO HE CAN BE **SEEN**, AND STRAPPED ON SOME HOME MADE JINGLE **BELLS**, SO HE CAN BE **HEARD** AND KEEP ANIMALS **AWAY!**

RED

KLING KLING -A- LING

KLING

HAND-MADE BEAR BELL STRAP

KLING KLING-A-LING

KLING KLING -A- LING

WILLY DID IT

KIDS, IF IT'S **HUNTING SEASON,** YOU CAN WEAR A **RED** SHIRT, TOO, TO BE **SAFE.**

COMMON SENSE

LONG AGO MY FATHER'S PEOPLE, THE CHEROKEES, LIVED IN THE SMOKY MOUNTAINS OF TENNESSEE, WHERE THEY HAD TO MAKE DO WITH WHAT THEY FOUND. THEY WERE SURVIVORS.

Willy DID iT

THEY HAD THE SPIRIT OF THE MOUNTAINS WITH THEM, AND THE TOWN OF CHEROKEE, NORTH CAROLINA, STANDS AS PROOF OF THEIR STRENGTH AND ENDURANCE. THEIR SPIRIT AND STRENGTH ARE ALIVE TODAY IN THE MORE THAN 17 MILLION PEOPLE WITH NATIVE AMERICAN BLOOD.   I HAVE SHARED THIS WITH YOU AND WITH MY GRANDCHILDREN.

So today, kids, it's good to know how to survive if you get lost in the outdoors. But even if you know how to use plastic bags instead of animal hides against the cold, or matches instead of a bow and drill for fire, what you need most of all is your COMMON SENSE. Remind grown-ups who take you on vacation into the mountains, woods, or desert to take plenty of jackets and blankets, and trail mix, and take plenty of water.

WATER is your LIFE! The old Cherokees used to drink about a quart of water in the morning, and this would last them all day until sunset.

WATCH the BIRDS and ANIMALS and LEARN. The wilderness was not wild to the Cherokees, it was HOME.

BE AT **PEACE** WITH THE **EARTH** IF YOU GO TO THE **GREAT OUTDOORS.**

LOOK, LISTEN, AND **THINK** AND YOU WILL MAKE IT **BACK SAFE!** IF YOU GET LOST, STOP FOR A MINUTE. LOOK AROUND YOU. THINK. TRY TO REMEMBER THE WORDS AND PICTURES IN THIS BOOK. YOU CAN DO IT! THE OUTDOORS IS FUN!

TREAT OUR **MOTHER EARTH** WITH **CARE** AND SHE WILL TAKE **CARE** OF YOU AND **PROTECT** YOU AND **GIVE** YOU **BEAUTIFUL** THINGS TO SEE.

See you on the TRAIL,

Willy WHITEFEATHER

WHAT DID YOU LEARN?

CHECK ONE ✓ ☐   ANSWERS AT THE BOTTOM

① YOU'RE IN THE HOT DESERT—WHAT DO YOU NEED MOST?

A ☐ A LIZARD   B ☐ WATER   C ☐ A BUCKET OF SAND

② YOU'RE IN THE MOUNTAINS IN WINTER—WHAT'S THE BEST THING TO HAVE WITH YOU?

A ☐ A BEAR   B ☐ A CAN OF BEANS   C ☐ HOW YOU THINK AND FEEL ABOUT YOURSELF

③ WHEN YOU'RE WALKING BY YOURSELF IN THE WOODS, WHERE DO YOU LOOK?

A ☐ DOWN AT THE GROUND   B ☐ AT WHERE YOU'RE GOING AND WHAT'S AROUND YOU   C ☐ UP AT THE SKY

④ YOU'RE IN THE MOUNTAINS AND A BIG CLOUD COMES IN... AND IT'S COLD AND DAMP AND YOU FEEL SLEEPY, SO WHAT DO YOU DO?

A ☐ GO TO SLEEP   B ☐ YAWN AND YAWN AGAIN   C ☐ JUMP UP AND DOWN TO GET WARM, THEN MAKE A FIRE

ZZZORK

EEYOWRAW

⑤ BEFORE YOU WALK AWAY FROM YOUR CAMP, WHAT DO YOU DO?

A ☐ LOOK TO THE NORTH, WHAT DO YOU SEE?   B ☐ LOOK DOWN AT THE ANT HILL YOU'RE STANDING ON   C ☐ LOOK AT YOUR BELLY BUTTON

ANSWERS ① - B ② - C ③ - B ④ - C ⑤ - A

IF YOU GOT 'EM ALL RIGHT, YOU'LL **MAKE IT!** CONGRATULATIONS!

FOUND SAFE!

A NOTE TO PARENTS AND GROWN-UPS

I HOPE YOU AND YOUR KIDS LIKE MY BOOK, AND MAYBE SOMEDAY IT'LL HELP YOU SURVIVE OUTDOORS IN AN EMERGENCY. GO OVER IT WITH THEM **CAREFULLY** TO MAKE SURE THEY **UNDERSTAND.**

ONLY YOU KNOW WHEN YOUR KIDS ARE READY FOR THINGS LIKE POCKET KNIVES, MATCHES, AND WATER PURIFYING TABLETS, AND IT'S UP TO YOU TO TEACH THEM HOW TO USE THESE PROPERLY—

SHARE THE GREAT OUTDOORS WITH YOUR KIDS. LEARN MORE ABOUT IT TOGETHER. IT WILL GIVE THEM CONFIDENCE AND SELF-RELIANCE, SO IF THEY GET LOST, THEY'LL COME BACK TO YOU SAFE!

IN FRIENDSHIP

Willy WHITEFEATHER

THE LAST PAGE

So Long

FOR INFORMATION ON CLASSES AND WILD PLANT IDENTIFICATION CARDS -

WRITE TO **LINDA RUNYON** • FEATURED IN PEOPLE MAGAZINE JULY 24, 1989

WILD FOODS CO. INC.

3531 WEST GLENDALE AVE. SUITE 369

PHŒNIX, ARIZONA 85051

OR CALL (602) 930-1067

SHE LIVED 17 YEARS IN THE MOUNTAINS, EATING THE WILD FOOD.

Reevis Mountain SCHOOL of SELF-RELIANCE *WILLY DID IT*

FOR BROCHURE ON CLASSES

WRITE TO **PETER BIGFOOT**

REEVIS MOUNTAIN SCHOOL OF SELF-RELIANCE • IN THE SUPERSTITION MOUNTAINS

HC02 BOX 1534

ROOSEVELT, ARIZONA 85545

OR CALL (602) 467-2536

BIGFOOT WALKED 85 MILES IN 15 DAYS ACROSS THE ARIZONA DESERT IN THE SUMMER OF '76, TAKING NO FOOD OR WATER, EATING THE WILD FOOD.